Produced by Kroha Associates, Inc.
Middletown, Connecticut.

Printed in the United States of America.

ISBN 1-56326-120-0

You're A Good Skate, Lilly

One cold, snowy day, Minnie and Lilly were playing checkers at Minnie's house when Daisy, Clarabelle, and Penny came running in.

"Guess what!" Daisy exclaimed. "There's going to be a winter festival at the park next Saturday!"

"There will be all kinds of contests," Penny added. "Building snowpeople, sled races, figure skating, and a skating relay race, too!"

"And they're giving prizes!" Clarabelle finished.

"I'm going to enter the sled race," Penny said. "And Clarabelle is going to build a snowlady!"

"And I'm going to enter the figure skating contest," Daisy added. "I've been taking ice skating lessons all winter, and I can do good figure eights and spins."

"Besides," she added, "I have a new blue skating outfit to wear, so I'll really look cute!"

"I know," Minnie said, joining in her friends' excitement. "Why don't we enter the skating relay race? We'd make a super team!"

"That's a great idea!" everyone agreed.

But Lilly shook her head. "I don't want to be on the relay team," she said softly. "You'll do better without me." She put on her coat and mittens. "I have to go now, Minnie," she said as she started to leave. "I just thought of something I forgot to do at home." Before anyone could stop her, Lilly was gone.

The next day after school, Clarabelle, Daisy, and Penny invited Minnie to go to the park to practice skating.

"I think I'll walk home with Lilly, instead," Minnie said. "I want to find out why she doesn't want to be on our relay team."

Lilly and Minnie walked together quietly for a while, catching snowflakes on their mittens and looking at the flakes' lacy patterns.

"You know, Lilly," Minnie said at last, "I'm sorry you don't want to be on our relay team. I'll miss having you as part of the fun."

"The truth is, Minnie, I don't know how to skate," Lilly explained, blushing. "And I'm afraid I'll embarrass myself in front of everyone."

"Not only that," she added, "I don't have any ice skates."

"I can teach you how to skate!" Minnie said. "It's not as hard as it looks — honest! And I even have some old skates in my attic that you can use."

"But what if I can't learn to skate well enough in time for the relay?" Lilly asked. "What if I look silly?"

"Don't worry about that," Minnie said. "Having fun is what counts."

"Well, all right," Lilly agreed at last. "I'll try."

Soon Lilly was in Minnie's attic, trying on a pair of pink skates. They fit perfectly!

"Now let's go to the rink for your first lesson," Minnie suggested.

When Minnie and Lilly got to the rink, Daisy, Clarabelle, and Penny were there. They watched as Minnie helped Lilly onto the ice. But when Lilly's feet hit the ice — BUMP — down she went!

Minnie helped Lilly stand up. Clutching Minnie's arm, Lilly slid forward a little. Lilly wobbled, but she stayed up. Slowly, she moved forward, getting better with each step. Then suddenly her left foot slid one way, and her right foot slid the other. OOMPH! Down went Lilly, with Minnie on top of her. A little girl skated past, giggling at them. Lilly got up.

"This is too embarrassing," Lilly said with a sigh. "I don't want to try anymore." She took off her skates and left the rink.

After Lilly left, Minnie and her friends walked home together.
"I guess Lilly's not going to be on our team for the relay," Penny said with a sigh.
"What if she won't even come to the festival?" Clarabelle said. "Even if she's not on our team, I don't want her to miss all the fun."

"Maybe Lilly thinks if she doesn't skate well on the relay team, we won't like her anymore," Minnie said.

"But Lilly doesn't have to be a good skater to be a good friend!" Daisy exclaimed.

"You're right, Daisy," Minnie replied. "And I'm going to go tell her right now!" Minnie and the other girls ran down the street to Lilly's house.

"Okay, Lilly," Minnie said when Lilly came to the door. "You don't have to skate on the relay team, but we still want you to come to the festival. It just won't be as much fun without you — and besides, you can cheer for us! Please come."

"Minnie's right," the others agreed. "We really want you to come."

Lilly smiled. "Okay," she agreed. "I'll be there — *if* I don't have to embarrass myself by skating!"

On Saturday, Minnie and her friends hurried to the festival. The
first event was building snowpeople. As Minnie, Daisy, Penny, and
Lilly watched, Clarabelle built a huge snowlady. She gave her orange
yarn hair and a big, pointy carrot nose.

But first prize went to a boy who had made a whole snow family,
complete with a snow dog!

"Aren't you embarrassed that your snowlady didn't win?" Lilly asked
Clarabelle after the prizes were handed out.

"Not really," Clarabelle grinned. "I had a good time making my
snowlady, and I think she's funny, even if she didn't win first prize."

The next event was the sled race. Minnie and her friends cheered as Penny sped downhill, gliding around the tall marker flags.

But just as Penny neared the finish line, her sled hit a patch of ice. It skidded one way, and Penny tumbled the other. She landed on her back in the snow as other sledders zipped across the finish line.

"You must feel silly about falling like that," Lilly said as she helped Penny brush the snow off her parka.

"Oh, that can happen to anybody," Penny laughed. "And anyway, it was fun!"

Soon it was time for the figure skating contest. "Look at Daisy!"
Minnie exclaimed as she and her friends watched Daisy skating on
one foot, making figure eights on the ice.

"I know Daisy's going to win," Clarabelle said. "She looks so pretty
in her new blue skating outfit!"

Then, right in the middle of a spin, Daisy stumbled and fell!

Afterward, her friends rushed up to her. "You must be so
embarrassed about falling like that," Lilly said.

"A little," Daisy agreed. "But not enough to stop trying. I'll do
better the next time."

Finally, it was time for the skating relay race. "Each team must have four different skaters," the referee said through a megaphone. "Each skater must go around the rink two times, then pass a red flag to the next skater on the team."

"Oh, I hope we win this time," Clarabelle said as she took the small red flag and got into her starting position. "This is our last chance to win a trophy!"

TWEET! The starting whistle blew. Clarabelle took off, skating as fast as she could.

"Go, Clarabelle, go!" Lilly yelled as Clarabelle zipped past her. In a few minutes, Clarabelle was around the rink a second time and handing the flag to Daisy.

"We're out in front!" Lilly cheered as Daisy sped away.

Penny was next in line. But as she tightened her skate laces, they broke! "Quick, Minnie, help me fix my laces!" Penny shouted.

"Hurry!" Lilly shouted. "Daisy's halfway around the rink!"

"I am hurrying!" Penny yelled as she tried to knot the broken laces.

"Quick, Lilly," Minnie exclaimed. "Put your skates on! You may have to take Penny's place!"

"Oh, no!" Lilly started to protest.

"Please, Lilly, we need your help!" Minnie urged.

Lilly gulped and started to put her skates on. *What if I fall? I'll be so embarrassed!* she thought as she tied the laces.

Suddenly Daisy was back, holding the flag out to Minnie. Minnie darted onto the ice. The crowd roared as she passed skater after skater. In a flash, Minnie was around the rink and starting her second lap.

"Penny, hurry!" Lilly yelled. "Minnie's almost back!"

"My laces keep breaking!" Penny shouted. "You'll have to skate for me, Lilly!"

"I can't!" Lilly wailed, but Penny pushed her onto the ice.

"You can do it, Lilly!" Minnie shouted as she pressed the red flag into Lilly's hand. "I know you can!"

Lilly's heart pounded. Her knees shook as she started off down the ice. *I won't think about being embarrassed,* she told herself. *I'll just think about skating as well as I can.* Lilly's knees stopped shaking. Her feet stopped wobbling. She skated a little faster, then faster and faster. She was halfway around the rink, then all the way around, then ...

"One more turn to go," Minnie and the others cheered.

Lilly kept skating. A skater in a green hat passed her, but Lilly kept going. A skater in red pants was coming up close behind, but Lilly kept going. The finish line was just ahead.

"Hurray for Lilly!" Minnie and the others whooped as Lilly glided across the finish line. She was just a few inches behind the skater in the green hat! "We won second place!" Lilly's friends announced as they dashed up to her.

Lilly could hardly believe it when the referee presented them with a shiny trophy for second place.

"Let's each take turns keeping the trophy," Daisy suggested.

"Okay," Minnie agreed. "But Lilly gets to keep it first! We couldn't have won without her. She's a good sport for trying — and a good skater, too!"

"Thanks, everyone," Lilly giggled shyly. "I hardly know what to do with all this attention. It sort of embarrasses me!"

Write and tell me about a time when you were embarrassed about doing something. Use the enclosed letter.